For Leo and Nina

www.apub.com
Amazon, Amazon Crossing, and all related logos are trademarks of Amazon.com, Inc., or its affiliates.
ISBN-13: 9781542008686 (hardcover)
ISBN-10: 1542008689 (hardcover)

The illustrations were rendered using mixed woodcut techniques with drawing and collage, as well as digital resources.

Book design by AndWorld Design
Printed in China

First Edition

10 9 8 7 6 5 4 3 2 1

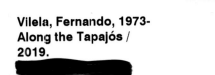

ALONG THE TAPAJÓS

Written and illustrated by
FERNANDO VILELA

Translated by Daniel Hahn

amazon crossing kids

We always wake up real early. We have banana porridge for breakfast, and when we hear the motor of Zé's boat in the distance, we grab our knapsacks and race over to the ladder.

It's time to go to school!

"Bye, Pa! Bye, Ma! Bye, Titi!"

Titi is our giant tortoise.

Living on the bank of a river is amazing, because
on the way to school there are so many animals!
Me and Zé love playing with the alligators.

Zé says there are lots of big creatures under the water that we don't even see and that they hang around real close to us, just waiting for somebody to jump in.

When the porpoises appear, Inaê makes a big fuss about them, and they leap around and put on an amazing show!

The boat takes us across the whole village.

"Is there some kind of celebration at the church tomorrow?"
I ask Zé.

"Yes," he answers. "There are going to be eight weddings. The priest
has come up from the city, and he's only staying two days."

Finally we get to school!

At the end of class, the sky turns dark.

"Winter's come!" somebody shouts.

Here in the state of Pará, we only have two seasons: summer and winter. In summer it's very sunny, it's very dry, and the river gets so shallow you can walk across it. But in winter it rains a lot, every day, nonstop.

Look at that rain!

We head back home in a downpour. Zé takes
everybody. The church is empty now, and the oxen are
getting onto the boat, ready for the big move.

Ma and Pa have already taken everything out of the house and put it in Uncle Pedro's boat—even my guitar.

"Hey, careful with that table! Get yourselves ready, kids— we're leaving in ten minutes!"

It's like this every year. When the first rains come, the whole village moves. People take everything: stools, tables, chickens, oxen, hammocks . . .

The only things they leave behind are the houses themselves.

Many hours later, the rain stops, and we reach dry land. We unload everything from the boat and put it on the oxcart— we still have a long road ahead!

In the middle of the rainforest,
Pa always finds a good spot, someplace
sunny and close to an *igarapé*—that's a
kind of waterway. Ma and Inaê arrange
our things and the food while Pa and I
fetch wood to build our house.

After the walls have gone up, the women gather a load of straw to make a roof, which we tie together nice and tight so that not a drop of water will come in.

That's when Inaê realizes we've forgotten someone.
"Ma," she cries, "we need to go back for Titi!"
"Too late now, child," says Ma. "Not till summer's come again."

That night, Inaê is sad. "Titi's going to starve, Cauã," she says to me,
"and he doesn't know how to swim! I wish we could go fetch him . . ."

So I think for a moment, and then I have an idea:
"Hey, I've got it—let's sneak out right now!"

The sun is just starting to rise as we untie the boat. We row all day long. At the end of the day, we arrive at the village.

When we reach the house, Titi is alive . . . on the roof.
But behind him there's a giant anaconda!

"Don't go, Cauã," cries Inaê. "The snake's going to eat you!"

"I've got to save Titi. He's going to die!" I say, climbing up onto the roof.

I don't know how it happens, but when I jump back into the boat with Titi in my arms, the queen of the jungle gets all tangled up!

So that's how we save Titi. He's happy, and we are even happier than he is. Of course, we don't know how mad our parents are going to be when they see us . . .

About the Tapajós River

The Tapajós (pronounced *ta-pa-ZHOS*) is one of the biggest rivers in the Amazon rainforest, stretching to a length of 1,200 miles (1,900 km). It's connected to the Amazon River by the Jari Channel, in the state of Pará, where this story takes place.

It's an area rich in fauna and flora: you can see alligators, hawks, snakes, all kinds of birds, trees up to 130 feet (40 m) tall, and giant water lilies.

Though it's always hot in the Amazon region, the people who live there call the rainy season (between December and May) "winter," and the low-tide period (June to November), when it rains less, "summer." When it does rain, there's just water, water everywhere! It rains nonstop! It rains so much that the river rises by more than 16 feet (5 m), flooding the houses and a good part of the rainforest—those areas of inundated Amazonian forest are called *igapós.* In the summer, when the water level drops back down, it's hard to get boats through the smaller tributaries of the rivers, known as *igarapés.*

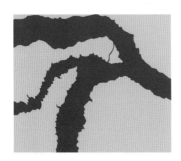

Many people live along the banks of the Amazon's rivers—they are called *populações ribeirinhas*, which means "riverside populations." Their day-to-day lives are totally different from those of people in the cities: they live in houses built on stilts, they sleep in hammocks, and instead of using cars and buses, they get around by boat. In the flooding season, a lot of people need to move, and even the schools get shut down. Children make the most of this time by playing soccer and having fun, just as in any other part of Brazil.

About the Journey

My thanks to Stela Barbieri, my flower and traveling companion

As a lover of the Amazon rainforest, Fernando Vilela got the idea for this book on one of his trips there:

"In July 2006, my partner, Stela, and I spent two weeks in Alter do Chão, a little fishing town on the bank of the Tapajós River. We befriended a fisherman called Rui who took us out on his boat to get to know the area. It was flooding season, and everything was underwater. Passing through the Jari Channel, we found a small riverside ghost town. We went into empty churches and empty schools. Everybody had moved away. Anyone with livestock had taken their animals with them. But there we were, on a boat ride through that overflowing world, where a lot of houses were only half-visible. In the Amazonian summer, though, it's a totally different sight. You arrive places by land, and the stilt houses on the banks of the rivers make up a really striking picture."